THIS BOOK
BELONGS TO

_____

_____

André Maurois

FATTYPUFFS

& THINIFERS

Illustrated by Fritz Wegner

VINTAGE BOOKS
London

Published by Vintage 2013

2 4 6 8 10 9 7 5 3 1

Text © 2006, The Estate of André Maurois, Anne-Mary Charrier,
Marseille, France
Illustrations © Fritz Wenger

Fattypuffs and Thinifers was first published in Great Britain by The Bodley
Head in 1941
Patapoufs et Filifers was first published in Paris in 1930

Vintage
Random House, 20 Vauxhall Bridge Road, London SW1V 2SA
www.vintage-classics.info

Addresses for companies within The Random House Group Limited can
be found at: www.randomhouse.co.uk/offices.htm

The Random House Group Limited Reg. No. 954009

A CIP catalogue record for this book
is available from the British Library

ISBN 9780099582922

The Random House Group Limited supports the Forest Stewardship
Council® (FSC®), the leading international forest-certification
organisation. Our books carrying the FSC label are printed
on FSC®-certified paper. FSC is the only forest-certification
scheme supported by the leading environmental organisations, including
Greenpeace. Our paper procurement policy can be found at

Contents

Contents

1

The Double Family

'HOW slowly you eat,' said Mr Double, who for some moments had been tapping with his fingers on the tablecloth.

'Not me, Father,' said Terry.

'No, not you, but your mother and your brother.'

It would have been difficult anywhere to find a more united family than the Doubles. Mr and Mrs Double were devoted to each other, and they adored their children. Their two little boys, Edmund and Terry, often quarrelled—after all, boys of nine and ten are not saints—but they couldn't get on without one another. Edmund used to say, 'Terry is always teasing me', but if Terry was away for two days Edmund was like a fish out of water; and Terry used to say, 'Edmund's too rough', but if Edmund happened to be ill Terry felt ill as well.

You never heard them say, as other boys do, 'I did this', or 'I saw that': they always said, 'We were at the Circus', or 'We had to go without our pudding', or 'We've had measles'. In fact, although there were two of them, they lived just as though they were one person.

But at meal-times the father and mother and the two boys did not get on quite so well. The Double family was divided into two halves. Mrs Double and Edmund, the older boy, were very interested in food. When he came back from school Edmund always went straight to the kitchen to find out what was for dinner. It was even said that at the age of eight months, when he was sitting at the table in his high chair, he had grabbed at a plate which someone passed just in front of him and clutched a chop in his little hand. Mr Double and Terry, on the other hand, never paid the slightest attention to what they were given to eat. All they wanted was to gobble it up quickly so that Mr Double could go back to his work and Terry to his toys. Both were rather thin.

'Edmund,' said Mr Double, 'if you go on eating like that you'll turn into a real Fattypuff!'

Mrs Double looked anxiously at her son. She herself was very afraid of getting fat, and since she could never resist sweet things she went for long walks and ran about the house all day to keep herself beautiful.

'What!' she said. 'Edmund isn't a bit like a Fattypuff!'

'Yes, he is,' said Terry, who loved teasing. 'Fattypuff! Fattypuff! Fattypuff!'

He said it so often that when they got down from the table Edmund gave him a punch, and he started to cry. As you see, the brothers simply couldn't get on without one another.

It was a Sunday in the summer, and Mr Double had promised to take the boys for a walk in the forest. These walks with their father were their greatest treat. If the weather was fine, Mr Double, after walking a mile or two, would find a nice, shady spot amid the rocks and trees. He would sit down with his back against a moss-covered stone and pull a book out of his pocket.

'I'll give you an hour,' he said on this particular day to his sons. 'You can climb the Twin Rocks and the Pointed Stone, only be careful! Keep within sound of my voice, and if I cry, "Hoi! hoi! HOI!" answer at once.'

'Hoi! hoi! HOI!' was the rallying cry of the Double family. They had a special way of making a long-drawn-out 'HOI' at the end, so that if they were in a crowd, or if it was dark, they could always find one another.

Edmund and Terry ran off. The Twin Rocks were two long flat stones leaning against one another, about eight or nine yards high.

'We'll each of us climb one side,' said Terry with an annoying grin, 'and I bet I get to the top before you do, old Fattypuff!'

'Terry,' said Edmund, 'if you keep on calling me Fattypuff I shall get cross, and then I'll hit you, and then you'll cry. You'd better start climbing the rock at once.'

Each of them went to one side of the Twin Rocks, and started climbing. It was difficult. You had to find places for your feet on the smooth surface, and places to grip with your hands. You had to go slowly. Edmund had climbed up about three yards when he heard: 'Hoi! hoi! HOI!' It was their father's voice.

Terry's voice replied, and from the direction of the sound Edmund guessed that Terry had already climbed higher than he. So he started to climb very fast, and he was just arriving at the summit when once again he heard a 'Hoi! hoi! HOI!' But this time it was a queer, stifled sound which seemed to come from amid the rocks. He had got so high that he could reach the top of the rock with his hand. He pulled himself up, and found

Hoi! hoi! HOI!

himself with his head hanging over the narrow opening between the Twin Rocks. For the third time he heard the cry of 'Hoi! hoi! HOI!' and then down below him, seemingly at the bottom of a sort of narrow chimney formed by the two rocks, he saw his brother.

'Terry!' he cried. 'What are you doing there? Did you fall?'

'No,' said Terry, who was too proud to admit it. 'I climbed down. Come and see, Edmund. It's lovely!'

'But what a long way off you are! What can you see down there?'

'There's a huge cave, and it's all lit up with electric lights, just like a railway station.'

'Are there any trains?'

There was nothing in the world Edmund liked better than trains.

'No. But it's awfully interesting. Come on down.'

'But how does one get down?'

'Oh, you just let yourself go. The ground's all covered with moss, and you can't hurt yourself.'

Edmund was not quite sure that he believed this, but he didn't want to seem afraid. He swung himself over the edge of the rock, hung by his hands, shut his eyes and let go. And down he went, sliding with terrific speed between the two rocks. Just for a moment he was frightened, but then there was a quite springy sort of bump, and he found himself seated on the moss beside his brother.

'Look!' said Terry.

It was a most surprising sight. An enormous grotto extended directly in front of them, filled with a bluish light which came from round, luminous balls hanging from its ceiling. The ground was covered with earthenware tiles, half of which were coloured red and white, and the other half blue and red. At the end of this grotto there was a large tunnel sloping gently downwards, from which came a rumble of machines.

'Why,' cried Edmund, 'there must be *people* living under the earth!'

'Of course there are,' said Terry. 'And do you know what there is in the tunnel?'

'What did you see?' asked Edmund.

'A moving staircase,' said Terry. 'Just like in the Underground.'

Edmund could resist no longer. He ran towards the tunnel. It was quite true! A moving staircase, so long that one could not see its end, was rumbling down into the centre of the earth. Beside it was another staircase going up, but there was no one on it.

'Let's go down!' said Terry.

'We ought to tell Father,' said Edmund.

'Never mind about that. We'll come straight back.'

Terry always wanted things so much that he never thought of the consequences.

At this moment they heard a very distant cry of 'Hoi! hoi! HOI!' They both replied 'Hoi! hoi! HOI!' at the top of their voices, and stepped on to the staircase.

2

The Two Boats

EDMUND and Terry would never have believed that a staircase could be so long. Down and down they went for more than an hour; down and down, through a half-darkness occasionally broken by red and green electric lights.

'It's just like the signals in the Underground,' said Edmund. 'But what a long way we've come!'

'Are you frightened, Fattypuff?' jeered Terry.

Edmund said nothing, and there was no sound except the rumble of the staircase—drum-bum—drum-bum—drum-bum—echoing in a vast stillness.

At length they saw, a long way below them, a semicircle of light such as one sees at the end of a tunnel. The semicircle grew larger; the light from outside shone on the walls of the tunnel, the lamps grew pale, and five minutes later the staircase deposited Edmund and Terry in a vast hall. At the foot of the stairs there were two soldiers with rifles. They looked funny, because one of them was short and very fat, and the other tall and very thin. The thin one said:

'Two Surface-dwellers. Two!'

The fat one answered:

'One Fatty and one Thinny. Two!'

Behind him a very thin clerk made two marks on a green sheet of cardboard. A fat man dressed like a railway porter came up to Edmund.

'What, no luggage?' he said, looking very astonished.

'No,' said Edmund. 'We're going straight back home.'

The fat man went away. A great many travellers were crossing the hall, and as they were all going in the same direction Edmund and Terry followed them. On the walls were large signs which said: 'To the Boats'.

The two boys were immediately caught up in the crowd. They passed through a doorway, and as they did so a fresh, cool breeze blew on their faces. They found themselves out in the open air and overlooking the sea, but although the light was very bright they could see at once that it was not sunshine. When they had had another look they discovered that the whole countryside was lit up by huge luminous balloons floating in the sky. These balloons were filled with a very bright blue gas, such as one sometimes sees in tubes outside shops. They gave a soft and pleasant light. A little town of bungalows and houses was clustered on the slopes leading down to the sea, and directly in front of the two boys was a harbour with a lighthouse and a jetty. Two gangways made of brightly shining metal connected two steamers with the quay. On one of the gangways there was a notice which read: 'Fattyport Line'. This gangway led to a big wooden paddle-steamer which was very broad and round. The other steamer, on the contrary, was made of steel, and was very thin and sharp. The notice on its gangway read: 'Line to Thiniport'.

'Shall we go for a sail?' said Terry.

'What will Father say?' said Edmund.

'We won't go far,' said Terry. 'It's quite a tiny little sea.'

Indeed it was more like a lake than a sea. By the light of the balloons one could see quite clearly an opposite shore, on which were tall houses.

'But we haven't any money,' said Edmund.

'Yes, we have,' said Terry. 'I've got two shillings left out of my pocket-money. Anyway, we didn't have to pay for the stairs.'

Edmund sighed and followed. He always ended by doing what his brother wanted. They walked side by side to the gangway which bore the notice 'Fattyport'. One of the ship's officers, a fat, red-faced man with a very big smile, pushed Edmund gently on board, saying:

'Hullo! A little Surface-dweller! It's a long time since we saw one of you.'

But when Terry wanted to follow, the officer said:

'Oh, no! You must go on the other boat.'

'But *we* always go together,' said Terry.

'On the Surface, perhaps,' said the officer. 'But you can't do that here. He's a Fattypuff and you're a Thinifer. There's no doubt about it. If you don't believe me you can weigh yourselves. There's a scale just over there. But hurry up if you want to take the other boat. It's just getting ready to start.'

At that moment the other boat blew several sharp blasts on its whistle. Terry never took long about making up his mind. He rushed to the second gangway, which

was just being pulled in, and in two jumps was aboard the second boat. Her engines had already started; the screws were churning up the water, and the sailors were casting off the mooring-lines. Amid all this noise Terry heard a voice crying, 'Hoi! hoi! HOI!' He ran towards the stern of the steamer and saw the other steamer making off in the opposite direction as fast as its big paddle-wheels could drive it. And there was Edmund, standing on a sofa and waving a handkerchief, with tears in his eyes.

Terry fumbled in his pocket, but could find nothing but a small and very crumpled bag of liquorice which he had bought the day before on his way home from school. So he waved the bag of liquorice. The other passengers looked at him in surprise, but he didn't mind that. He was very unhappy at being separated from his brother. What would become of him, now that he was all alone and surrounded by strangers?

3

The Thiniport Line

WHEN Edmund was no more than a tiny speck in the distance Terry sighed lightly and looked about him. He had often crossed the sea before: he had been across the Channel, and he had even been to Marseilles and Algiers; but he had never been on a boat like this one. All the other boats he had been on had plunged up and down from bow to stern (his father had told him that this was called 'pitching') as well as from side to side (which was called 'rolling'). It was the rolling which had made Terry seasick. But this boat didn't do any rolling: it was so long and thin that it only pitched. Terry felt quite comfortable, and he was very hungry.

All sorts of things were happening on deck. Everybody seemed to be walking or running or giving orders. Numerous hawkers were going about carrying little

trays loaded with newspapers, books, magnifying-glasses, watches and tape-measures. Terry hoped that one of them might also be selling chocolates or bananas, but not one of them sold anything to eat.

Through the windows of the saloon he could see a lot of men doing gymnastics. Some were lifting heavy weights; others were throwing a ball to one another; and others, seated in mechanical boats, were pulling away as though they were rowing. It all made Terry think of the windows of the big shops at Christmas-time, when they are full of mechanical figures which never stop moving.

But soon he was struck by something even more surprising. Although there were such a large number of people aboard, there wasn't a single one who was fat, or even moderately plump. All of them—men, women and children—were dreadfully, dreadfully thin. One could see the bones through their cheeks. There was no flesh on their hands, and their clothes hung loosely about them.

In spite of this they did not seem in the least ill. On the contrary, they appeared to be in the best of health, and extremely active and vigorous. But it was plain that this was a most peculiar race of people, and almost unbelievably thin.

'Where am I?' Terry wondered. He thought of all the people he had seen on his travels, but he couldn't think of a country where all the people were thin. And anyway, he had never heard of a country that you reached by going down a moving staircase.

He walked up and down the deck, thinking this over; and presently, as he passed a door on which were the words 'WRITING ROOM', he noticed a large map in a frame. He examined it with growing surprise, because it was not in the least like any map he had ever seen, and it did not contain a single name he knew.

He examined it for a long time. Although he had been third out of thirty-seven in Geography he could not remember anything at all about this strange country. And while he was racking his brains, an elderly, white-haired, very thin gentleman stopped beside him and gazed at him sternly.

'Aha!' he said. 'From the Surface?'

'Who, me?' said Terry.

'Yes, you! You came down the stairs, didn't you?'

'Yes,' said Terry, '*we* did.'

'Precisely,' said the elderly gentleman. 'Exactly what I said, from the Surface. Down here we don't understand your Surface countries, where you mix fat and thin people without making any difference between them. Under the earth the races are properly separated. There are Fattypuffs and there are Thinifers.'

'And I suppose the Fattypuffs are all fat, and the Thinifers are all thin,' said Terry.

'Intelligent child!' said the old gentleman teasingly. 'He has grasped it all by himself! Ten marks out of ten.'

He was a sarcastic and unpleasant old person, but Terry wanted to find out where he was, so he continued the conversation. He learned that his companion was called Mr Dulcifer, and that he was Professor of History at the Thinifer National Academy. It would, in any case, have been easy to guess that he was a professor, because he was always asking questions.

'Name the capital of Thinifer,' he said suddenly.

'Who—me?' said Terry.

'Of course, you. There's no one else, is there?'

'We—' said Terry, 'we've learnt Italy—capital, Rome; Poland—capital, Warsaw; Hungary—capital, Budapest. But no one ever taught us about Thinifer.'

'Nought,' said Mr Dulcifer. 'Repeat after me: the capital of Thinifer is Thiniville.'

Terry repeated this.

'Now then—the capital of Fattypuff?' said Mr Dulcifer.

'I'm not sure,' said Terry. 'Is it Fattyville?'

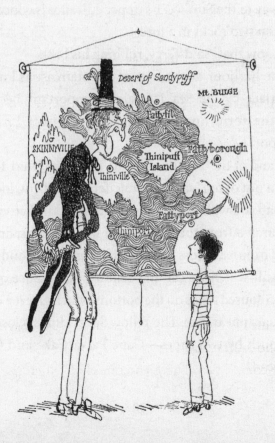

'Five out of ten,' said Mr Dulcifer. 'Repeat after me: the capital of Fattypuff is Fattyborough.'

'Well, that's easy to remember!' said Terry. 'I only wish the capital of Sweden was Swedeville, and the capital of Greece, Greekborough.'

'Silence!' said Mr Dulcifer. Drawing Terry in front of the map, he continued: 'The staircase by which you arrived, which links the two races in the centre of the earth with the people on the Surface, is known as the Stairway to the Surface. Its upper entrance is concealed between two rocks in a forest.'

'I know that,' said Terry, rubbing his back.

'The harbour at the foot of the staircase is known as Surface-by-the-Sea. It is highly important, because it is the terminus both of the Fattypuff Line to Fattyport—'

'—and of the Thinifer Line to Thiniport,' said Terry.

'Ten out of ten,' said Mr Dulcifer. 'Now if you look at the map you will see that the Kingdom of the Fattypuffs is separated from the Republic of the Thinifers, first by a land frontier, across the Desert of Sandypuff, and then by a gulf which we call the Yellow Sea, because of the gold-coloured rocks on the bottom, which give it a quite unusual appearance. The Yellow Sea is almost closed in the south by two capes—Cape Pat-a-Cake and Cape Nailhead.'

'I see,' said Terry. 'And in the middle there's an island called the Island of Thinipuff.'

'Exactly,' said Mr Dulcifer. 'And I wish that island were at the bottom of the sea, because it is the cause of all our troubles.'

But before going on with Mr Dulcifer's history and geography lesson, we really ought to see what was happening to Edmund . . .

4

The Fattyport Line

WHEN Edmund found himself alone on a strange ship, when he saw Terry disappear over the horizon, and thought of their poor father, who by this time was probably anxiously searching for them, he nearly burst into tears. How he longed to be safely back at home, playing with his train! But he knew very well that a boy of ten must not be a cry-baby, so he pulled himself together and tried to understand what was going on around him.

At first he was afraid of being seasick. But when he had crossed the Channel it was always the pitching which had made him feel ill; and this ship didn't pitch, it only rolled. So he began to feel very well and very hungry.

The deck was crowded with arm-chairs, in which ladies and gentlemen were asleep. Some of these arm-

chairs were made of leather, others of canvas, and still others were rocking-chairs which rocked gently to the gentle movement of the waves. The sailors did not have arm-chairs, but they strolled casually about, some with their hands in their pockets, and others eating bits of bread and chocolate, or perhaps a piece of sausage or the wing of a chicken. Up on the bridge was the captain. He was seated in an arm-chair with a table beside him laden with cakes and things to drink.

Everybody—captain, sailors and passengers—looked happy and good-humoured; but the extraordinary thing was that every single one of them was fat. Edmund had met, among his parents' friends, quite a number of plump ladies and gentlemen, but he had never before seen such a gathering of people with round tummies, huge pink cheeks, fat hands and such a general air of contentment. Since he remained standing, an old lady with at least four chins beckoned to him.

'You're a little Surface boy, aren't you?' she said.

'Yes,' said Edmund cautiously. 'I suppose so.'

'Of course you are,' said the fat lady. 'I could tell at once you were from the Surface. But all the same you're a real Fattypuff, and of the best type.'

'I'm nothing of the kind!' said Edmund furiously. 'My father——'

The sound of his voice had awakened some of the sleepers. An old gentleman with a white beard, whose tummy was about two yards round, and who was dozing in a red arm-chair decorated with gold, opened his eyes and looked about him.

'What's the matter?' he asked.

'I beg your pardon, your Excellency,' said the fat lady, with great respect. 'This little Surface boy seems quite surprised because I told him he was a real Fattypuff.'

'My young friend,' said the old gentleman kindly, 'you should be proud of being a Fattypuff, particularly at a time when your brother Fattypuffs have just covered themselves with glory.'

'Who are my brother Fattypuffs?' demanded Edmund, in a voice which was still rather cross.

'Tut, tut!' said the old lady. 'Don't you know that you're talking to the Chancellor, Prince Vorapuff? You should call him "Excellency".'

The old gentleman smiled indulgently.

'Bring me the map,' he said.

When it had been brought he showed Edmund a map exactly like the one Terry had looked at, except for one difference: the island in the middle of the gulf, which on Terry's map was called the Island of Thinipuff, was here called the Island of Fattyfer.

After Edmund had studied it for some time the Chancellor said gently:

'And now, my young friend, I am tired and must finish my nap. But don't run away. I'll get them to bring you a chair, a few biscuits and a history book, in which you will be able to read everything you need to know before landing.'

He said a word to a young secretary, who brought Edmund a book which he regarded with some suspicion.

But while Edmund was looking dubiously at this volume, a fat sailor approached. After putting down a small table on which was a steaming cup of cocoa and bowls of fruit and cakes, he pulled up an arm-chair.

Edmund found this snack so tempting that he sat down, drank a sip of cocoa, ate a mouthful of cake and opened the book, reflecting that the Fattypuffs certainly knew how to live.

The first page of the book was as follows:

The Puffs. Invasion by Fattys. Plumpapuff I. 1023–1407.

1. In olden times our country was called Puffia, and its inhabitants were known as Puffs. The Puffs were as renowned for their strength as for their gentleness. Although they were divided into numerous tribes they never fought among themselves or with their neighbours. The Puffs had no king: each tribe elected a chief who was also the High Priest.

2. About the year 800, the first of the race of horsemen known as Fattys appeared from the north, in the Desert of Sandypuff. The Fattys were as violent as the Puffs were easy-going. Although less numerous they attacked the Puffs, occupied all the country north of Puffia, and there founded the town of Fattyborough which at first was their fortress.

3. Thanks to their gentle way of life the Puffs easily endured the domination of their new masters; and from the mingling of the two races there emerged the race of Fattypuffs, who were at once as gentle as the Puffs and as brave as the Fattys.

4. In the year 1023 a grand assembly of the chiefs of the Fattys and the Puffs resolved to recognise as their king Plumpapuff I, who was the son of a Fatty chieftain and a young Puffian princess. At the same time the two united nations adopted the name of Fattypuffs and made Fattyborough their capital.

Edmund had got as far as this when the fat sailor returned, smiled at him, took away the cup of cocoa which he had just finished and put in its place a big bowl of soup and some cheese straws.

'Something more to eat?' said Edmund, quite timidly.

'Luncheon isn't for another hour,' said the sailor. 'One has to keep one's strength up.'

Edmund, who was very fond of soup, made no further protest. He leaned back in his chair and this time turned to the end of the book.

'As I'm just going to arrive in their country,' he thought, 'I suppose I ought to know the latest things that have been happening.'

This was the beginning of the last chapter:

Plumpapuff XXXII. (1923–19..) New Demands by the
Thinifers. War of the Captive Armies, 1928. Treaty of
Fattyfil, 1929.

1. King Plumpapuff XXXII, who succeeded his
father in 1923, after the glorious death of the latter in
the middle of a tremendous meal, is one of the most
remarkable monarchs yet produced by his illustrious
family. Never have the Fattypuffs had a fatter or a
kinder king. Upon his accession the palace gates and
the larders of the royal kitchen were thrown open to the
people, and the tax on Turkish delight was abolished as
a thank-offering. Under this king the Fattypuffs might
have known perfect happiness had it not been for their
neighbours, the Thinifers. . . .

'Thinifers?' thought Edmund. 'That's like the word
which was written on the boat Terry was on. . . . Who are

the Thinifers?' he asked the fat sailor, who had remained near him.

'Ah!' said the sailor, slowly and sadly raising his arms to the sky. 'The Thinifers? . . . I will tell you. But first, if you don't mind, I'll go and fetch myself an arm-chair.' He returned a few moments later bearing an enormous sandwich, which seemed to be stuffed with lobster salad and hard-boiled eggs, and a glass of beer, and dragging a large arm-chair in which he seated himself next to Edmund.

'The Thinifers,' said he, pausing after each sentence to refresh himself, 'are an extraordinary race who inhabit the opposite side of the gulf. They are horrible to look at, being excessively thin, bony as skeletons and yellow as lemons. They live in the most ridiculous way. They scarcely eat anything, they drink nothing but water and they even work without being made to. But all that wouldn't matter if they weren't so downright nasty. We Fattypuffs are so easy-going that we can put up with anything; we don't even mind people being different from ourselves. But the Thinifers want to force everybody to live as they do. For example, in the middle of the gulf there is a pretty little island called Fattyfer. You'd scarcely believe it, but two years ago the Thinifers had the cheek to try and force the inhabitants of the island (who are almost real Fattypuffs) to obey their absurd laws, which meant going without lunch and working six days a week. They made such a fuss about it that the wretched inhabitants appealed to us for help, and we had to defend them.'

'Was there a war?' asked Edmund.

'What!' exclaimed the fat sailor in great surprise. 'You mean to say you didn't know! Why, it was the most terrible war that has ever been known in the countries under the Earth. It was called "The War of the Captive Armies".'

'Why the "Captive Armies"?'

'Because the two armies, as you'll see if you read the history book on your knee, both ended by being taken prisoner.'

'How on earth did that happen?'

'You read it out,' said the sailor. So Edmund read aloud:

'3. Since earlier wars had shown that it was impossible for an army to cross the desert of Sandypuff, the Fattypuff General Staff decided to attack the coast of Thinifer by sea. The army, under the command of the gallant Marshal Puff, embarked on May 15th. The landing was a complete success. The land of the Thinifers was conquered without the slightest difficulty, and on June 3rd Marshal Puff entered Thiniville.

'4. By an unfortunate coincidence, on the very same day General Tactifer, commanding the Thinifer army, made his entry into Fattyborough. For some months the Thinifer General Staff had been secretly collecting stores and means of transport in order to cross the desert of Sandypuff; and since this was not defended their enterprise had, unfortunately, been completely successful.

'5. But when the Thinifers, having conquered Fattyborough, began to consider the problem of returning to their own country, they realised that in crossing the desert they had lost nearly all their tanks and lorries. Moreover, they had no fleet. In fact, although they were conquerors, they were also prisoners, because they had no means of getting back.

'6. At the same time the Fattypuff fleet, which had been treacherously lured out to sea off Cape Matapuff, was wrecked in a gale on the rocks known as the Iron Needles. So the Fattypuff army was also a prisoner—in Thiniville. That is why this campaign came to be known as the War of the Captive Armies.

'7. In these circumstances the two countries had no alternative but to sign an armistice. King Plumpapuff and President Bonifer met at sea, off the frontier town of Fattyfil, and agreed upon the following terms:

(*a*) That the Island of Fattyfer should remain neutral;

(*b*) that sea transport for the return of the two armies should be arranged;

(*c*) that a conference should be held at Fattyfil the following spring to settle matters of detail.

'8. The army, under the command of Marshal Puff, returned at the beginning of October and was received in triumph. The Senate of Fattyborough besought King Plumpapuff XXXII to accept henceforth the title of Plumpapuff the Victorious, and Marshal Puff was made Duke of Thiniville.'

Having finished the book Edmund closed it and drank his soup, which was excellent.

5

The Thinifers at Home

'THAT island,' said Mr Dulcifer, 'is the cause of all our troubles.'

'Why?' asked Terry.

Mr Dulcifer took a little book out of his pocket and handed it to him.

'History of the Thinifers,' read Terry. 'No,' he said, 'I've never read it. The only books I've read are *Alice in Wonderland, The Wind in the Willows, and Twenty Thousand Leagues Under the Sea.*'

Mr Dulcifer opened the book at one of the last pages and said crossly:

'Read it!'

Terry obeyed and read this title.

CHAPTER LIV

President Bonifer (1925–19..) Outrageous Demands of the Fattypuffs. War of the Captive Armies. Treaty of Fattyfil.

'The Fattypuffs?' he said. 'Who are the Fattypuffs?'

'The Fattypuffs,' said Mr Dulcifer, 'are an absurd nation who live on the opposite side of the gulf. They are horrible to look at, fat as balloons, soft as cushions and red as tomatoes. They are as lazy as cats. They eat and drink, and above all sleep, the whole day long. The worst of it is that if they were allowed to go on behaving in this disgraceful fashion they would spread their abominable habits through all the countries under the earth. For instance, in the middle of the gulf there is this little island called Thinipuff. You would scarcely credit it, but two years ago the wretched inhabitants, who are real Thinifers at heart, were so shocked by the behaviour of the Fattypuffs (who went there for their holidays) that we were obliged to go to their defence.'

'Was there a war?' asked Terry.

'What!' exclaimed Mr Dulcifer furiously. 'Do you mean to say you didn't know? It was the greatest war in history, the one which has since been called "The War of the Captive Armies."'

'Why "Captive Armies"?'

'Because the two armies, as you will find out for yourself if you will pay proper attention to the book I have placed in your hands, both finished by being made prisoners.'

'How did that happen?' asked Terry.

'Read,' said Mr Dulcifer severely.

And Terry read:

'3. Despite the peaceful intentions of our government, General Tactifer, the Commander-in-Chief of the Thinifer Army, had for many years studied the means of carrying out an enterprise which had hitherto never been successfully undertaken: the crossing of the Desert of Sandypuff. Within three weeks he had arrived at the gates of Fattyborough.

'4. Unfortunately, on the same day a Fattypuff army disembarked on the coast of Thinifer and entered Thiniville. A just retribution awaited the invaders: their fleet, attacked by the sailors of Thinifer, was destroyed in the waters around the Iron Needles. The Fattypuffs were thus prisoners in the land they had conquered.

'5. But General Tactifer most regrettably was unable to take advantage of the perilous situation of the Fattypuffs. The truth is that the Thinifer Army, in the course of its superb crossing of the Sandypuff Desert, had lost nearly all its transport. It was therefore unable to leave Fattyborough. Hence the name given to this campaign—The War of the Captive Armies.

'6. An armistice signed in the Bay of Fattyfil on July 12, 1928, authorised the repatriation of the combatants. The Thinifer Army, under the command of General Tactifer, returned towards the beginning of October, and was received in triumph. The General returned to his native village of Skimpton Parva, where he may still be seen guiding his own plough.'

At this moment the history-reading was interrupted by a long blast of the siren. Terry ran to the rail and uttered a cry of surprise. Before him lay a big harbour, whose houses were high and narrow as towers. Many

of these towers were ornamented with sculpture. They were built of stone of a pinkish grey, and the effect was most charming. The flag of the Thinifers, red and blue in the shape of an oriflamme, was to be seen everywhere. Indeed, Thiniport would have been the most beautiful of towns if so many of its towers had not been in ruins.

'The damage was done by the guns of the Fattypuff fleet,' said Mr Dulcifer.

Thanks to Mr Dulcifer, Terry had no difficulty in getting through the Customs, although the officials were very strict with travellers who had no passport. Their waist and chest measurements were taken; they were weighed, and those whose weight was greater than was considered correct at their age were mercilessly refused the right to enter the country. From a printed notice hanging on the wall Terry saw that at nine years he should weigh less than forty pounds, and should not be more than twenty-four inches round the chest. But he was as thin as any Thinifer, and was accepted at once.

Mr Dulcifer took him with him on the train from Thiniport to Thiniville. The train was quite comfortable, but naturally it was very narrow, because four Thinifers only took up as much room as two Surface people, or one single Fattypuff. The houses in the country were all like towers, less high than those at Thiniport, but quite different from houses in ordinary countries, because the rooms were all placed one on top of the other.

The poplar seemed to be the favourite tree, and the greyhound the favourite dog.

'Oh dear!' thought Terry as he examined the odd little train. 'How happy Edmund would be if he were here! He's always so keen on collecting new sorts of railway coaches.'

But Edmund must be a long way off by now; and Terry was more sorry than ever when Mr Dulcifer said:

'We're getting close to Thiniville.'

Soon Terry saw the houses of a huge town.

6

Lord Chancellor Vorapuff

EDMUND was just as astonished by his first glimpse of Fattyport as Terry had been when he arrived at Thiniport. The houses at Fattyport were as plump and round as the Thiniport houses were tall and pointed. All the buildings in Fattyport were surmounted by domes and cupolas, and they were enclosed in walls curved just like a human stomach, which, as Prince Vorapuff explained to Edmund, was generally held to be the most splendid invention of the Fattypuff architects.

Thanks to the Chancellor, Edmund had no difficulty about going ashore. He simply had to submit to the formality of being weighed. Since he was ten years old he was expected to weigh not less than seventy pounds, but he weighed seventy-three, so everything was all right.

He was almost speechless with delight at the things he saw. Everywhere there were enormous, round Fattypuffs who seemed to be brimming over with contentment and kindness. All down the passage-way leading to the platform were shining nickel tubes bearing labels such as 'ORANGEADE', 'FIZZY LEMONADE', 'STRAWBERRY MILK-SHAKE', 'COCA-COLA', and all the most beautiful drinks you can imagine. Beside each tube was a big pile of paper cups, and all you had to do was to press a button to fill one of them with the drink you preferred. Little girls went round selling the most enormous cakes. The Fattypuff chocolate éclairs were almost as fat as motor-tyres, and the cream-buns were as big as bath-sponges. But unfortunately Edmund had no money. Besides, he had to follow Prince Vorapuff, and so he dared not stop.

He could not help giving a cry of rapture as he saw the train. It was enormous. The rails were about five yards apart, and huge bulging coaches overhung the track on either side. Prince Vorapuff invited Edmund into his private coach and gave him a splendid compartment all to himself, saying that he personally was going to do a little work next door. Well, that was certainly what he said . . . but a little later Edmund heard him snoring.

A very fat head-waiter entered Edmund's compartment and offered him a long menu illustrated with the most beautiful drawings.

'Will your Lordship be so kind as to order lunch?'

Very pleased at being so respectfully addressed, Edmund took the menu and read:

MARAPUFF OYSTERS

❧❧

PUFF SOUP

❧❧

LOBSTER FATTYBOROUGH

❧❧

FATTYPUFF STEAK

He stopped reading when he had got this far, and asked:

'How many courses am I allowed to have?'

'Why—as many as you like,' said the head-waiter, much surprised.

Edmund ate all the way to Fattyborough, and gazed through the window at the rolling meadows filled with huge, sleek cattle, most of them asleep. He liked the round farm-houses, like balloons, where the Fattypuff farmers lived. And balloons seemed to be the Fattypuff children's favourite toys. You could see them everywhere, and as the train drew near to Fattyborough the air was filled with them. Some of them were lighted up. Below them the plump, round houses were illuminated by the street lamps. It was lovely.

'Well!' thought Edmund. 'I'm certainly going to like being here!'

But all the same he felt terribly lonely. He thought of his poor father, who at that moment was probably

hunting everywhere round the Twin Rocks in search of his two boys. If only he could come down too! If only he could find the staircase! It would be grand if suddenly one were to meet him.

'But the trouble is,' thought Edmund sadly, 'Father's certainly a Thinifer, and that means he'd have to go on the other boat. He'd find Terry all right, but not me. It doesn't look as though I shall see any of them any more....'

But Edmund couldn't be sad for long. The more he got to know the Fattypuffs, the more he liked them. You couldn't imagine nicer people. They were never cross, and they never said unkind things about one another. They were scarcely ever unhappy. Nearly all day long they laughed and played and made jokes, and most of their conversations were about food. They had a meal every hour, and then they slept for a quarter of an hour—which was known in Fattyborough as the hourly snack and the hourly nap. The only thing that ever put them in a bad humour was the wickedness of the Thinifers. But when one saw the ruins which the Thinifer invasion had left everywhere in their pleasant countryside, one could not feel surprised at this.

In any case, although they had so many reasons for being cross, all that most of the Fattypuffs wanted was to live on friendly terms with their neighbours.

'It is true,' they said, 'that the Thinifers are people one can hardly be expected to understand, seeing that they don't like eating or drinking or laughing. But all the same, just because two nations have different tastes, that is no reason why they should shoot things at one another, and wound people and burst their balloons.' All the Fattypuffs hoped that the Conference of Fattyfil, which was soon to take place, would put an end to their differences for ever.

'But why have you been fighting each other for so long, you and the Thinifers?' Edmund one day asked the son of Prince Vorapuff.

'Well, you know,' the young man said, 'it's so silly that I hardly like to tell you. The fact is, we really quite agree with the Thinifers that it's far better that the Island of Fattyfer should not belong to either of us. It might be dangerous for the Thinifers if it belonged to us, and it might be dangerous for us if it belonged to the Thinifers. But the Thinifers, although they don't mind its being independent, want it to have the name of Thinipuff; and we want it to be called Fattyfer.'

'But what difference does it make?' asked Edmund.

'It doesn't make any difference at all to me,' said young Vorapuff, whose name was James, 'or to anyone else, really. But my father says that the honour of the Fattypuffs makes it impossible for us to give way.'

'Well, then, what are you going to do?'

'I've already told you. It has been decided that in a month's time three representatives of the Fattypuffs and three representatives of the Thinifers will meet at Fattyfil, which is on the frontier. And then they'll try to agree. That's what you call a conference.'

'We have conferences on the Surface,' said Edmund. 'We've had no end of conferences—in fact, so many that people stopped paying any attention to them.'

'My father says that it's much better if people don't pay any attention to them,' said James Vorapuff. 'But this is our first conference and the Thinifers take everything so seriously.'

After a time Prince Vorapuff chose Edmund for his secretary. Edmund had always been first in writing at school, but he had never thought how useful this would be to him in the future. It was a particularly interesting job because it enabled him to get to know all the most important people in the kingdom—the Head Cook, the Chief Pastrymaker and the Supreme Cigar-maker. He was even presented to His Majesty King Plumpapuff XXXII.

'Don't forget,' said Prince Vorapuff, 'you must call him "Sire" and "Your Majesty".'

But when he found himself in the King's presence Edmund was so astonished at the size and roundness of the Royal stomach that he could not remember a single one of the polite things he had meant to say. Quite without meaning to, he blurted out:

'Humpty-Dumpty—I mean, Your Majesty . . .'

But fortunately King Plumpapuff, like his subjects, was a person of great good humour, and he only laughed very loud. He chatted to Edmund for five minutes about cooking on the Surface. Sometimes he had Surface meals himself, and he promised Edmund that he would invite him one day to a Surface dinner.

'It will remind you of your country,' he said kindly.

At this moment a Fattypuff officer in a magnificent gold-embroidered, red uniform entered the Audience Chamber. His chest was entirely covered with decorations, of which it took an enormous number, because it was

almost as big as a feather-bed. Prince Vorapuff, who was standing behind Edmund, whispered:

'That is our greatest soldier: Marshal Puff, Duke of Thiniville.'

'Good day, Marshal,' said the King. 'Are you getting ready to go to Fattyfil?'

'I do not yet know,' said the Marshal, 'if Your Majesty will do me the honour of sending me there.'

'What!' said the King, 'it would be a fine thing if the man to whom we owe the Peace were not sent to discuss its terms! Was it not,' he continued, turning to Edmund, 'a Surface warrior who said: "His has been the suffering, his shall be the honour"?'

'Yes,' said Edmund blushing. 'I think it was Joan of Arc.'

'Sire,' said the Marshal solemnly, 'I swear to you that there can be no happier day in the life of a Fattypuff soldier than the one on which he is able to sign a lasting peace.'

'I'm sure of it, Marshal,' said the King. 'Let us drink to Peace.'

The Grand Steward instantly brought in a bottle of champagne as high as a man, which was wheeled on a little trolley, and emptied it into an enormous gold tankard. The King and the Marshal drank in turn, in the Fattypuff fashion, gazing into each other's eyes. Edmund thought it a very nice ceremony. He would have liked it even more if they had given him a little of the champagne.

'Marshal,' said Prince Vorapuff, when the King had withdrawn for his siesta (for His Majesty, unlike the rest of his subjects, found it necessary to have a nap every half-hour), 'you would, perhaps, like to have a little chat with my young friend on Surface methods of warfare. He has been telling me the most interesting things about the holes they dig in the Surface countries in order to protect themselves from shell-fire.'

'I've heard about that,' said the Marshal. 'In fact I even sent a secret mission up the Stairway to the Surface in order to study these holes, which I believe are known as trenches. But they wouldn't suit us, I'm afraid. For one thing, Fattypuff soldiers would need such very wide trenches that they'd scarcely be any protection at all. And then, as Your Highness knows, the Fattypuffs greatly dislike digging. What they like is a nice, short fight—it may be a bit dangerous, of course—and then, if they're still alive, a good hearty meal and a sleep. I'm sure you'd be interested,' he went on, turning to Edmund, 'in our special line of field cookery. For instance, have you ever tasted woodcock baked in clay?'

And for the rest of his visit he talked of nothing but food.

As secretary to the Chancellor, Edmund saw all the preparations which were made for the Conference of Fattyfil. He greatly admired the good-will of the Fattypuffs. They were ready to agree with the Thinifers about everything—except, of course, that the Island of Fattyfer should be called Thinipuff. But Edmund himself was beginning to feel that they were right about this.

Everybody in Fattyborough was so sure that the conference would be a success, and that a real Peace would be signed, that all the highest dignitaries of the State hoped to be sent to Fattyfil. But there could only be three members of the delegation, and when the list was published in the newspapers many people were disappointed. Fortunately the Fattypuffs were not ambitious, and by the time they had had a good meal all the disappointment was forgotten. The list of delegates was as follows:

The Chancellor, Prince Vorapuff.

Marshal Puff, Duke of Thiniville.

Professor Ramfatty, President of the Academy of History.

Professor Ramfatty had been chosen because he knew more than anyone else about the history of the Island of Fattyfer, on which he had written a hundred and twenty-three volumes. The Chancellor thought that his vast knowledge would come in handy if the Thinifers should raise this question again. But most people in Fattyborough were sorry that he had been chosen, because he was considered to be rather bad-tempered. He was descended from one of the very few families which were known in Fattyborough as 'pure Fattys'.

You could tell these Fattys by their names, which always ended in 'fatty' instead of in 'puff'; but they were even more easily known by their characters, for nearly all of them still retained something of the primitive violence of the early conquerors of the land. Like all the Fattypuffs, they were fat, but their faces were different from those of the other families. The Thinifers always said that it was important to distinguish between the 'sheep-Fattypuffs' and the 'boar-Fattypuffs'. The 'boar-Fattypuffs' were the 'pure Fattys'. They formed a highly respected aristocracy in this country, which attached the greatest importance to birth. But it did not seem to be a very happy choice for a conference which was intended to bring about peace and conciliation. However, it was hoped that the well-known mildness of the Chancellor, and the unshakeable pacifism of Marshal Puff, would keep the fiery professor under control.

On the eve of their departure for Fattyfil, Prince Vorapuff told Edmund that he had chosen him out of all his secretaries to accompany him to the conference. Perhaps he was rather proud of having a secretary who came from the Surface.

7

President Rugifer

WHILE Edmund was becoming so popular with the leading Fattypuffs, Terry was getting to know the Thinifers.

They were remarkable people in many ways. For one thing, they worked much harder than people on the Surface. Terry had been accustomed to see his father

Man must eat to live
not live to eat

relax a little while he drank his coffee after lunch: he
would chat with his wife or play with his sons. But no
one had ever seen a Thinifer over the age of thirty play
any kind of game; and when the young people played
ballgames (with curiously-shaped, narrow, oval balls),
they did it with an earnestness which made it seem like
a kind of drill.

It seemed that for the Thinifers the most valuable thing
in the world was time. When they made an appointment

they named the time exactly, to the very second. They arranged to meet each other, for instance, at 6 hours 17 minutes 3 seconds, or 3 hours 14 minutes 22 seconds. At the home of the Dulcifers the two daily meals were at eight sharp in the morning and eight sharp in the evening, and if the children had not taken their place at table by the last stroke of eight they went without. As for the mid-day meal, no one any longer had such a thing. The Thinifers always ate standing up. They ate very little and very fast. You never saw a confectioner's shop in the towns, but only shops selling things like spaghetti and adding-machines. At the beginning of each meal Mr Dulcifer would stand in front of his empty plate and in a stern voice repeat the following words, which he said had been written by a great Surface-dweller: 'Man must eat to live, not live to eat.'

The Thinifers were wonderfully good at arithmetic, and everybody in Thiniville kept accounts all the time, never overlooking a penny. Their money was in the form of pieces of gold and silver and copper wire of different lengths. When a lady in a tram paid two pieces of copper wire for her fare, she immediately got out a little notebook and wrote it down. She had to do this standing up, because there were no seats in the trams. Even the richest man in the country, Mr Plutifer, the President of the Thinifer Spaghetti Corporation, always

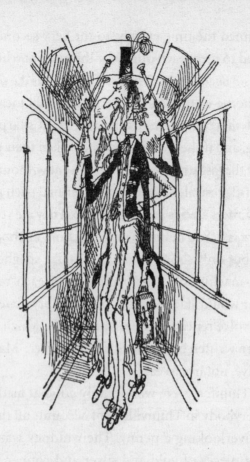

travelled standing up in his car, because the Thinifers
considered that to make yourself comfortable was a sign
of weakness. There were never any lifts in the houses,
although they were so extremely high, and Terry got
very out of breath climbing the narrow staircases with
their high steps.

Making spaghetti was the Thinifers' principal industry, but they also made sausages and candles. They were very much hampered by their intense dislike of anything round. For instance, they did not make wheels and motor-tyres themselves, and so were forced to buy these from the Fattypuffs. On the other hand, the Fattypuffs bought long, thin things—such as piston-rods and steel-wire (and, of course, spaghetti)—from the Thinifers.

It is not surprising that in a country where so much attention was paid to accuracy, things were inclined to work rather better than they do on the Surface. Terry had often heard his father and mother become exceedingly cross when they tried to get a number on the telephone. But with the Thinifers, the person you wanted to talk to you was there almost before you gave the number. Trains came and went punctually down to the very second. School-children did exactly the same lessons, at the same moment, in every school throughout the country. And Terry liked this exactness on the part of the Thinifers. At least you always knew where you were.

But unfortunately, despite their many virtues, they were not nice-natured people. They were not really cruel or evil, but envious and ambitious. No sooner did one Thinifer have something than all the rest wanted it. In the streets you constantly saw people quarrelling. Mr

Dulcifer was always saying unpleasant things about his fellow-professors. The Dulcifer children were jealous of one another, and if you were friendly with one, the other two immediately became sulky. Their parents were very strict with the children. They punished them constantly, and never ceased to say that it was for their own good.

Mr Dulcifer explained to Terry from the start that he could not send him to school with his own children because he saw no reason why he should pay for his education.

'You must earn your keep if you want to stay here,' he said. 'It's for your own good.'

'But what can I do?' asked Terry.

'Plenty of things. For instance, your handwriting is quite good. You might become a secretary.'

'What is a secretary?'

'A secretary is a person who writes letters for another person, and who makes notes for them—in short, who assists them in their work.'

'But I hate writing letters,' said Terry.

'I didn't ask you whether you liked it or not,' said Mr Dulcifer. 'Among us Thinifers if you want to eat you must work. It's for your own good. I shall go into the matter in the morning, and find out whether there's a vacancy in any of the Government offices.'

The next day when Mr Dulcifer came home he said he
had found a job for Terry with President Rugifer, who
had long been looking for a secretary from the Surface.
At the mention of President Rugifer, Mrs Dulcifer and
the young Dulcifers uttered cries of astonishment.

'What a bit of luck!' they said to Terry.

'Who is President Rugifer?' Terry asked.

'He is the President of the National Council,' said Mr
Dulcifer solemnly, 'and the Minister of Slimming.'

'Please—what does that mean?'

'President Rugifer,' said Mr Dulcifer, still in a very solemn voice, 'is one of our greatest men. He has succeeded in making every citizen lose nearly five pounds in weight, and in reducing our rations by twenty per cent. He is expecting you tomorrow morning at 6.33.'

'Me?' said Terry. 'But I never get up before seven!'

'Well, my young friend,' said Mr Dulcifer, 'you will have to change your habits. Perhaps it will console you to reflect that by gaining one hour a day one gains 365 hours a year and 21,900 hours in sixty years. In other words, one lives an extra 1,825 days. You see, it's for your own good.'

But the next morning, although he got up before daylight, Terry arrived a few minutes late at the Ministry of Slimming. The commissionaire at the door, who was a model of slimness, consulted his notes. 'Terryfer?' he said. 'Terryfer! Ah, yes! . . . But, miserable boy, you were instructed to be here at 6.33 and it is now 6.37! You'll get a warm welcome from the President!'

He picked up a telephone, and Terry could hear a strange voice roaring over the wire. At a sign from the commissionaire he followed him along a corridor scarcely a yard wide to a door covered with leather. The door opened and Terry saw, seated at a desk, a man who

looked almost like a knife-blade. But although he was so thin as to be very nearly invisible he had a tremendous voice.

'Are you Terryfer?' he bellowed. 'You're a sluggard and an idler!'

'But—' said Terry.

'Silence! You are a half-wit and a nincompoop!'

'I'd better try to keep quiet,' thought Terry, 'and perhaps he'll calm down.'

He soon discovered that this was the best thing to do. In fact, if you did not answer back, Mr Rugifer calmed down at once. In order to relieve his feelings he found it necessary to say two insulting words to anyone who had annoyed him; but he never said more than two, and these were enough to terrify the Thinifers. He was not really by any means a bad-natured man. In fact, he was better than most of his fellow-countrymen, and when Terry had grown accustomed to his ways he became quite fond of him.

Terry's work was not difficult. All he had to do was to answer the telephone and say, 'I am sorry, but the President is engaged.' It was a bit monotonous, but Terry had always liked telephoning. At the end of the week he was quite used to President Rugifer and did not take the slightest notice when he said, 'Terryfer, you are a half-wit and a nincompoop!' He came to take this as much for granted as if the President had simply said 'Good morning'.

There were two nice things about President Rugifer: he loved his country and he loved Mrs Rugifer, who often came to his office. She was pretty and gentle and much less thin than the other Thinifer ladies. If he had dared, Terry would almost have said that she was a Fattypuff.

But President Rugifer would have been furious if he had done so, because he hated the Fattypuffs more than anything in the world.

'They are cut-throats and vermin!' he said.

But all the same, he adored Mrs Rugifer.

8

The Conference at Fattyfil

TO GO on a journey with Prince Vorapuff was always extremely pleasant. Huge cars on balloon tyres took the Fattypuff delegation, with Edmund among them, to the little harbour of Fattybeach. Here the Royal Yacht was waiting, placed at their disposal by His Majesty King Plumpapuff XXXII. All the boats in the harbour were

decorated with flags, and great streamers were spread across the quay bearing the words: 'Long live Peace! Love to the Thinifers!'

No sooner had the yacht set out over the golden waves of the Yellow Sea, with all the members of the delegation settled down in large arm-chairs, than a waiter appeared with a menu bearing the classic words:

MARAPUFF OYSTERS

∽◦∾

PUFF SOUP

∽◦∾

LOBSTER FATTYBOROUGH

∽◦∾

FATTYPUFF STEAK

and everybody ate steadily, without wasting a moment, all the way to Fattyfil. Everybody, that is to say, except

Professor Ramfatty, who delivered a lecture on the Island of Fattyfer, explaining how it had been colonised by the Fattypuffs. The captain of the yacht rather riskily took his ship within a few yards of the northern coast of the island, so that they could see the inhabitants on the foreshore, all waving handkerchiefs. The little town of Fattyfil was decorated with flags in the colours of both nations. A guard of Fattypuff and Thinifer soldiers, in comical contrast, received the disembarking visitors with full military honours. Five minutes later the Thinifer delegation arrived, punctual to the minute. It was composed of three members:

His Excellency, Mr Rugifer, Prime Minister and Leader of the Delegation.

General Tactifer.

Professor Dulcifer.

Edmund watched them get out of the train with a great deal of curiosity. The cramped Thinifer railway line, with its long, narrow coaches and its rails so close together, was particularly fascinating to him because of his fondness for railways. He was also very interested in studying the signals, which were divided at the frontier into two distinct kinds. On the Fattypuff side they were round, with red and green circular lamps, whereas on the Thinifer side you saw thin streaks of blue or yellow light. But suddenly Edmund turned, and, despite the solemnity of the occasion, uttered a cry of joy and astonishment. Getting out of the train, just behind the three important Thinifer gentlemen, was his brother!

'Terry!'

'Edmund!'

They both ran round the outskirts of the gathering to clasp each other's hands. Although they did their best to keep quite calm, so as not to attract too much attention, they had never been so happy in their lives. Prince Vorapuff, who had been watching them, asked for an explanation. When he learned that his secretary was the brother of Mr Rugifer's secretary he was moved nearly to tears, and he remarked to Mr Rugifer that this extraordinary coincidence must certainly be a good omen for the conference. Mr Rugifer replied coldly that it was a matter of no importance.

The first meeting between the two delegations was not very encouraging. For some months workmen from both countries had been busy building a special Conference Hotel, exactly on the frontier. It had not been possible to entrust the design of this building to an architect from one of the Underground countries, because the country whose architect was not chosen would have been certain to be very cross about it. So a young architect from the Surface had been chosen instead. But although he had designed a very nice building, which people on the Surface would have liked, neither the Fattypuff nor the Thinifer statesmen were at all pleased with it.

'Much too flat,' said Professor Ramfatty, with disgust.

'Much too heavy,' said General Tactifer contemptuously.

When they got inside they found things even worse. The architect, utterly bewildered by the contradictory orders he received, had finished by building his hotel just as he would have done on the Surface. The revolving doors in the main entrance gave rise to painful incidents. The Thinifers, being so slightly built, had the greatest difficulty in making them turn at all; and when they did succeed they found themselves being whirled round and round because they could not get them to stop. As for the Fattypuffs, they had hard work in squeezing themselves in, and still more in getting out.

Terry and Edmund were delighted to find stairs and lifts such as one sees on the Surface, but they were the only ones who admired them. The Fattypuffs, who were accustomed to have moving staircases everywhere, thought them absurdly small and narrow. The Thinifers rushed at the stairs in their usual hurried fashion, but since these were differently shaped from their own a number of them fell down. Professor Dulcifer grazed his knee and became more irritable than ever, and Marshal Puff, who had had several of his medals scraped off in the lift, panted and grumbled.

In fact, Terry and Edmund realised in the first few minutes that everything was going wrong. The delegates began to tell each other in reproachful voices that the conference had been extremely badly organised. The Fattypuffs had proposed that before starting work they should have a little meal together. But the Thinifers, who never ate anything in the middle of the day, insisted on holding the first session immediately. Prince Vorapuff, alarmed by the terrible voice of Mr Rugifer, agreed at once, but he ordered a great pile of sandwiches and cakes so that he would be able to bear up under the strain of missing his usual meals.

Finally, the two delegations sat down together round a large table covered with a green cloth, in the biggest reception room in the Town Hall. Edmund and Terry, standing behind their respective chiefs, made little friendly signs to one another. Prince Vorapuff was just about to propose that they should elect a chairman, when Mr Rugifer got up and said in his unfriendly way:

'Before we begin our discussions there are two points about which I wish to make myself perfectly clear, in order that there may be no misunderstanding. First, I consider it is extremely bad taste that Marshal Puff should be described in the list of delegates, which has been circulated to the Press, as the Duke of Thiniville. Marshal Puff never captured Thiniville: it was Thiniville that captured Marshal Puff.'

Edmund looked at his poor friend, the Marshal, who became exceedingly red in the face and was about to reply when Mr Rugifer continued:

'Secondly, we cannot agree that the island which is the subject of these discussions should be referred to by the name of Fattyfer, since from time immemorial it has been known as the Island of Thinipuff. We know very well that when the delegation opposite changes the name by putting "Fatty" first they do so because they want to make it seem that the island belongs more to the Fattypuffs than to the Thinifers. But I shan't let myself be tricked like that. This second point is to be considered as an ultimatum. We shall not continue the discussions a minute longer unless it is settled immediately.'

The Fattypuffs, all of them with their mouths full, looked at each other in consternation. Professor Ramfatty seemed furious. He whispered something in the ear of Prince Vorapuff, who said:

'I call upon Professor Ramfatty to reply in the name of the King of the Fattypuffs.'

'Gentlemen,' said Professor Ramfatty, 'we should be able to understand President Rugifer's feeling in this matter if the name of Fattyfer were a new one. But this name is as ancient as the history of our two countries. In the twelfth century, in the works of our great poet, Shakespuff, you will find the immortal line:

  "Island of Fattyfer with blossoming almond-trees..."

'In the thirteenth century——'
Prince Vorapuff, seeing that Mr Rugifer was about to burst out, interrupted with a smile:

'Gentlemen, in order to show our desire for conciliation, let me make the following proposal. We will call it the Island of Fattyfer, and the Thinifer delegation will call it the Island of Thinipuff. And so nobody will be offended.'

Mr Rugifer reddened in his turn.

'I never heard a more insulting proposal! Professor Ramfatty is a pedant and an ignoramus.'

The Professor turned blue in the face, then white and then a fiery red. He coughed, choked and left the room. Prince Vorapuff and Marshal Puff looked at one another and then followed him, not knowing what else to do. The Thinifer delegation promptly left by the opposite door. The room was empty except for Edmund and Terry, who rushed towards one another.

'Are your Thinifers quite mad?' asked Edmund.

'No,' said Terry, 'but you've got to know old Rugifer. He's not a bad sort, really. When he said that Ramfatty was a pedant and an ignoramus he was being almost polite—for him. He'd have calmed down in another minute, if Ramfatty hadn't got cross.'

'What a pity!' said Edmund. 'If you knew the Fattypuffs you'd understand. They're so gentle and friendly. They've come here simply wanting to make peace.'

'Well, you'll have to try and explain to them what I've just been telling you,' said Terry. 'And you'd better do it quickly or there'll be trouble. I know the Thinifers. They're not difficult to get on with, really, but there's nothing they won't do if you rub them up the wrong way over their national pride. I heard them say in the train that they'd sooner start the war again than accept the name of Fattyfer.'

'Don't you think it's idiotic?' said Edmund.

'It's pretty silly,' said Terry. 'But if we could only arrange things——'

'There might be a way,' said Edmund. 'Supposing everybody were to agree that while the conference is on they'd call it the "Island of Fattyfer or Thinipuff".'

Terry thought for a minute.

'Yes,' he said. 'I think I could get President Rugifer to agree to that. Let's hurry!'

Edmund entered the room into which the Fattypuff delegation had withdrawn and found the three stout old gentlemen seated round a table eating their hourly meal. He told them of the conversation he had just had with his brother.

The poor Marshal was still exceedingly upset by the things Mr Rugifer had said about him.

'I never asked for the title of Duke of Thiniville,' he said plaintively. 'I'm quite willing to give it up.'

Prince Vorapuff did his best to console him, and assured Edmund that he would gladly agree to call it the 'Island of Fattyfer or Thinipuff.'

But when Terry made the same proposal to Mr Rugifer he instantly replied:

'If you think I'd ever call it by such a name you're an idiot and a blockhead!' Then, after a moment's reflection, he said more calmly: 'Well, perhaps I might agree to call it the "Island of Thinipuff or Fattyfer".'

'If it's only a question of which order they're in we ought to be able to come to an agreement,' thought Terry.

He ran back to the room where the Fattypuffs were. But now to his great surprise, he found them as obstinate as the Thinifers.

'Certainly not!' said Professor Ramfatty. 'It's out of the question! We should never be able to return to

You're an idiot and a blockhead

Fattyborough. The young people would stone us in the streets!'

At this moment a soldier entered bearing a message from President Rugifer. It was to say that the proposal which he had sent by his secretary was the last he would make, that it was an ultimatum, that he gave the Fattypuffs ten minutes to accept it and that he had ordered his train and would leave immediately if his wishes were not complied with.

'This means war!' said Marshal Puff in despair.

'War!' repeated Professor Ramfatty with satisfaction.

A quarter of an hour later the Fattypuffs arrived once again on the quay, still stunned by the disaster. So intense had been their emotions throughout the proceedings that they had missed two of their hourly siestas, and their eyes were almost closed with weariness. Edmund gazed admiringly after the snaky little train, on its narrow-gauge lines, which bore the Thinifers back to their own country.

9

Renewed Warfare between Fattypuffs and Thinifers

NOTHING could have surpassed the enthusiasm with which Mr Rugifer was received in Thiniville. President Brutifer, although quite pale with jealousy, came to meet the delegation. All the young people of the town swarmed into the streets along which the three heroes had to pass on their way to the Ministry of Slimming. Even the poorest citizens had bought flags, and long pennants flew from the tops of the thin towers. In all the public squares military bands played the special 'Hymn to Slimness' composed by the great musician, Flutifer. And notices were already being posted up ordering the Army and Navy to mobilise at 5.34 sharp the next mormng.

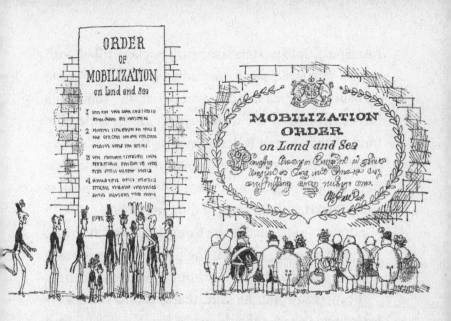

Nothing, I repeat, could have surpassed the enthusiasm of the Thinifers, unless it was the reception accorded to Professor Ramfatty and his colleagues at Fattyborough. King Plumpapuff even went so far as to postpone one of his hourly meals in order to receive at the foot of the Palace steps the delegates who had so nobly upheld the honour of the Fattypuffs. Ladies of the oldest families came in person with bouquets of flowers. Professor Ramfatty, who had taken the firmest attitude at the conference, was the most warmly praised—a remarkable fact, when one considers how gentle the Fattypuffs were as a rule. The choir at the Chapel Royal sang the 'Hymn to Plumpness', composed by the great musician Tumski-

Korsapuff. Bill-posters, carrying buckets filled with vanilla-flavoured paste, immediately started to paste up balloon-shaped notices of mobilisation ('some time before the end of the week') which all the little boys immediately began to lick. Perhaps they would have licked less eagerly had they known all the troubles that were to be brought upon them by those pink posters surmounted with the flags of the Fattypuffs.

Edmund took part in the Council of War, at Prince Vorapuff's house, at which the plan of campaign was decided. Marshal Puff was brimming with confidence.

'I can assure you,' he said, 'that this time the enemy forces which cross the desert of Sandypuff will find themselves up against something when they debouch on to the Plain of Fattypuffia. Not only shall I concentrate the entire army on the fringe of the desert, but I've got the Labour Corps, much as they hate labour, to promise to dig those curious protective ditches, known as "trenches", which have been described to me by the highly intelligent young Surface-dweller who is with us at this moment.'

Everybody looked at Edmund, who blushed with pleasure.

'The difficulty about these trenches, as the Surface-dwellers dig them,' continued the Marshal, 'is that they are much too narrow for an ordinary Fattypuff to be able to get into them. On the other hand, the wider they are the less use they are as a protection. But the head of the Corps of Engineers, General Sappapuff, has invented a sort of globular trench, narrow at the top and rounded at the sides, which solves the problem. The only objection to it is that it can only be entered at either end, so that it is not possible to make a mass sortie. However, as we intend to fight a purely defensive war, this is of no importance. On the contrary.'

Prince Vorapuff warmly congratulated the Marshal and announced that the King had created him Prince of Sandypuff. He added that the young Surface-dweller, to whom the Fattypuffs might well owe their salvation, would henceforth be known as Baron Edmund of the Staircase.

Meanwhile Terry was attending the Thinifer Council of War, under the Presidency of Mr Rugifer.

'I declare the meeting open,' said Mr Rugifer, 'and I call upon General Tactifer to outline his plan of campaign.'

'Gentlemen,' said General Tactifer, 'war being essentially the art of surprise, there can be no question of repeating the strategy which was so successful last year. Three facts must be borne in mind:

'1. The Fattypuffs no longer have a fleet. They have not been able to rebuild the one which was destroyed on the Iron Needles. Therefore they could not offer any serious opposition to an invasion by sea.

'2. For the same reason, we ourselves have no need to fear invasion.

'3. The Fattypuffs being slow thinkers, always prepare for the last war. It is almost certain that they will lie in wait for us on the edge of the Sandypuff desert.

'I therefore propose: (*a*) That an expeditionary force should be sent to occupy the Island of Thinipuff, because it's always a good thing to have something up one's sleeve.

'(*b*) That our main army should be transported to a point on the Fattypuff coast as near as possible to Fattyborough, which we shall then attack.'

'General,' said Mr Rugifer, 'you are a strategist and a warrior. What do you want? The country will give it you.'

'I want,' said General Tactifer, '198 ships each capable of carrying 1,003 men.'

'Make a note, Terry,' said Mr Rugifer. Terry took a sheet of paper and made hurried notes, at the General's dictation, of the number of lorries, guns and aircraft which he required. He was a little alarmed because from time to time the General paused to ask him some such question as:

'If you can get 32 men into a lorry, how many lorries do you need to carry 198,594 men?'

And when Terry did not answer at once:

'You're an ignoramus and a nitwit,' said Mr Rugifer.

'If I ever go back to school,' thought Terry, 'I shall be top at mental arithmetic.'

A fortnight later the Thinifer Expeditionary Force disembarked with complete success on the Fattypuff coast.

Terry had never seen war before, but after seeing this one he never wanted to see another. He heard the shells going W-H-I-I-I-Z over his head and suddenly exploding with a terrific C-R-U-M-P. He saw his Thinifer friends cut in halves by fragments of steel (although they were so thin that there was scarcely anything of them to hit). In the evening he heard aircraft zooming over the camp, and for the first time in his life he realised that an aeroplane was not always something to look up at and admire.

As they advanced he saw villages destroyed by gunfire, women and children wounded, little boys who had lost both father and mother. The poor Fattypuffs had not a chance of resisting. Nearly all their soldiers were in the north, on the edge of the Sandypuff desert, waiting in their globular trenches for an enemy who would never come.

Marshal Puff tried to bring some of his army south as quickly as possible, but they had the greatest difficulty in getting out of the trenches. Moreover, the Fattypuffs had never been very rapid movers. The unhappy regiments, arriving one by one, could do nothing except die bravely. The army of the Thinifers, on the other hand, operating with marvellous precision, reached the outskirts of Fattyborough in a fortnight.

Marshal Puff engaged in one last battle under the walls of the city and was taken prisoner with all his troops. It was a sorry spectacle when the old warrior, his head bowed, surrendered his sword to General Tactifer.

Despite his harshness the General was so moved that he had the happy thought of causing his vanquished adversary, whom he saw to be extremely hungry—for not a morsel of food had passed the Marshal's lips for more than an hour—to be served with a meal worthy of a Fattypuff.

Meanwhile Terry was searching everywhere among the prisoners for his brother Edmund, but he could not find him.

'Oh, dear!' thought Terry. 'Supposing Edmund has been killed!'

Next day General Tactifer's army entered Fatty-borough. The town which had always been so happy was now in mourning. Even the cake-shops were closed. The ladies were clothed in black. Prince Vorapuff, who was extremely pale and had lost two stone in the past fortnight, received General Tactifer and his staff at the gates of the Palace. Terry, who was following the conquerors on horseback, saw Edmund standing behind him, crying. He would have liked to go and console him, but he wasn't a very good rider, and he was afraid that if once he got off his horse he would never be able to get on again. As soon as the ceremony of surrender was over he ran to his brother.

'Why are you looking so miserable?' he cried. 'You're not really a Fattypuff.'

'I know,' said Baron Edmund of the Staircase. 'But I've got used to them.'

This time the Thinifers were pitiless. A telegram came from President Rugifer announcing the Peace Terms. King Plumpapuff XXXII and the whole land of the Fattypuffs, together with the Island of Thinipuff, were annexed by the Thinifer Republic.

10

The Thinifers in the Land of the Fattypuffs

THANKS to Terry, who did everything he could for his brother (for he had a kind heart although he seemed not to care about things), Edmund was given a job in General Tactifer's office. At first he refused, because he did not wish to forsake his Fattypuff friends, but the Fattypuffs themselves advised him to accept. They were adaptable people, easily resigned to their lot. Having been beaten, they attempted only to preserve their national customs.

At first they found it very difficult to get used to the ways of the Thinifer Army of Occupation. For instance, when a colonel in the Thinifer army summoned you to an interview at five minutes past eight it really did mean five minutes past eight; but for a Fattypuff it meant any time between eight o'clock and midday. So naturally they did not find it altogether easy to understand one another.

Then again, the matter of rations gave rise to great difficulties. The huge army which had to be fed caused a shortage of food, and at the start the Thinifer authorities tried to compel the Fattypuffs to give up their hourly meals, but this, as Mr Rugifer might have foreseen, was absurd and impossible. The Fattypuffs were gentle creatures, but if you deprived them of their food they turned savage. General Tactifer soon saw that his army would be in danger if he stirred up a general revolt throughout the country.

There were some servile Fattypuffs who, hoping to obtain favours from their conquerors, went into special slimming establishments in order to make themselves thinner. One saw advertisements in the papers like this:

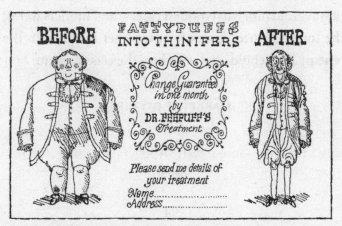

BEFORE · FATTYPUFFS INTO THINIFERS · AFTER

Change Guaranteed in one month by DR. FEEPUFF'S Treatment

Please send me details of your treatment

Name.........................
Address.........................

But the people who tried these methods only made themselves ill; some of them even died. In any case they ran the risk for nothing, because a thin Fattypuff was not in the least like a genuine Thinifer. His skin hung in absurd loose folds, and he was rightly despised by all the loyal Fattypuffs.

Moreover, events very rapidly took an unexpected turn. The Thinifer officers and soldiers billeted with the inhabitants found the Fattypuff cooking excellent. Terry, who ate at General Tactifer's table, perceived a gradual change in the commander.

'After all,' said the General, 'I am bound to study the customs of the country I have conquered and have now to administer.'

The truth was that he was beginning to take a fancy to a diet which was so much nicer than the one to which he had been accustomed. Edmund laughed like anything one day when, having been invited by Terry (who had always told him what modest eaters the Thinifers were), he found Prince Vorapuff's own chef installed in the enemy household, and with him the classic menu:

MARAPUFF OYSTERS

∾∾

PUFF SOUP

∾∾

Although he had been dethroned, King Plumpapuff still had some influence over General Tactifer, who often went to ask his advice.

'He's a man like any other,' said the General. 'But he's reasonable, and his views are worth hearing.'

The King was very clever at saying things, without sacrificing his dignity as a Fattypuff, which pleased and touched the General.

'I should be the last, General,' he said, 'to compare your military virtues with those of the gallant Marshal Puff, who is an old servant of my House and for whom I have the deepest affection. You are two men of very different types, each equally deserving of admiration. But if I had had an organiser such as yourself at the head of my armies, who knows whether I should not still be King of the Fattypuffs? Perhaps no one but General Tactifer could vanquish General Tactifer!'

'Really, you know,' said General Tactifer to Terry, as they departed from the interview, 'the old boy's quite intelligent!'

He became more and more well-disposed towards the Fattypuffs. At the same time Terry perceived that the

Thinifer army was becoming gentler and more indolent in its ways. A number of Thinifer soldiers married Fattypuff girls, and the army returned to Thiniville with feelings of real friendship for the people it had conquered.

Terry was very astonished by the change in the Thinifer Republic when the army returned. People's habits, their ideas and conversations all seemed to him different from what they had been only a short while previously. He took his brother to Professor Dulcifer, who agreed to lodge the two of them for a small sum. But his house, which had been so characteristically Thinifer, was now scarcely recognisable. From the first Terry had warned Edmund about the importance of punctuality, and that he must be down for breakfast on the first stroke of eight. But, incredible as it may seem, the young Dulcifers were not there. Mr Dulcifer drummed impatiently on the tablecloth (and this made Terry and Edmund think of their father—where was he now?). Finally with a sigh he murmured the ritual phrase: 'One must eat to live and not live to eat,' and began his breakfast.

The young Dulcifers did not arrive until ten minutes later, when their father had finished.

'Where have you been?' demanded Mr Dulcifer in a terrible voice.

'In our room,' said the children calmly, without even apologising.

'What!' cried Mr Dulcifer furiously. 'You have the insolence to arrive ten minutes late, although you heard the clock strike eight!'

'Who cares?' said the young Dulcifers. 'People don't make all that fuss in Fattyborough.'

It was a trifling incident, but similar happenings were taking place in every household. The truth was that many Thinifers had learnt during the war that there was a gentler way of living. The soldiers' wives, rendered envious by the tales told by their husbands, demanded a law making it legal to open cake-shops. The school-children demanded that they should have the right to buy cakes and sweets as they did in the schools

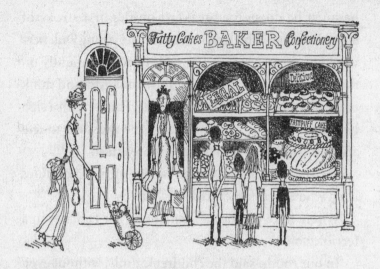

in Fattyborough. The soldiers in barracks wanted to be able to stay in bed till eight, as the Fattypuff soldiers did.

'These post-war customs are atrocious,' said Mr Dulcifer, 'and they are all the more dangerous because the moment is approaching when we shall have to make a decision upon which the whole future of our country will depend. You know that we have annexed the Kingdom of the Fattypuffs and the Island of Thinifer?'

'Yes,' said Terry.

'So far, so good,' said Mr Dulcifer. 'But are the Fattypuffs to be regarded merely as a subject race, or are they to become our fellow-citizens? Will they vote like the Thinifers? Will they make laws like the Thinifers? You can understand that if we let them vote, since there are more of them than there are of us, they will introduce into our country their greed, their plumpness, their Plumpapuff and all their abominable customs.' At this thought Mr Dulcifer grew visibly thinner, and wrung his long, bony hands. 'Their plumpness and their Plumpapuff!' he repeated. 'Intolerable!'

As it was thirteen minutes past eight he then departed.

'Well, as for me,' said Edmund to Terry, 'I hope they do allow the Fattypuffs to vote. It would do them good to change their habits in this rotten country.'

'Why?' said Terry, who had Thinifer instincts.

'Because I've been half starved ever since I've been here. Two meals a day! Look, my clothes are simply hanging on me!'

Alas, it was true! Really worried about his brother, Terry ventured the next day, when he went to work at the Ministry, to question Mr Rugifer as to the future.

'What!' said Mr Rugifer. 'What's that? You're a Paul Pry and a chatterer!'

'You see, sir,' said Terry, who was no longer afraid of him, 'it's because of my brother. You see, although he comes from the Surface he's——' he hesitated.

'Well?' said Mr Rugifer. 'Well, what is he?'

'He's a bit inclined to be a Fattypuff. And since he's been here he's been most awfully hungry.'

He repeated their conversation with Mr Dulcifer.

'Dulcifer,' said Mr Rugifer, 'is a fool and a coward. When one is sure of one's country, as I am, one has no hesitation in allowing everyone complete liberty. I cannot say any more at present, but—you have seen Rugifer at war: you have still to see Rugifer at peace.'

He said no more, but it was enough to enable Terry to guess that the influence of Mrs Rugifer was making itself felt, and that the President was favourably inclined towards the Fattypuffs.

11

Fattypuffs and Thinifers

O N THE eve of the plebiscite Mr Rugifer made a great speech which was broadcast to every corner of the country, even to the thinnest villages.

'Henceforth,' he said, 'Fattypuffs and Thinifers must form one single nation. Why should there be these

absurd distinctions as to weight and waistline? Can truth only exist if it weighs less than ten stone? Must all plump people be wrong? Is that your policy? It is not mine! Look at the Surface-dwellers. There you will find parliaments of Thinifers presided over by a Fattypuff Prime Minister. You will find Fattypuff husbands living happily with Thinifer wives. Let us imitate them. Let us form a new power, which will be invincible, because it will be the only one—the United States of the Underground!'

The enthusiasm with which this speech was received proved that many Thinifers shared the sentiments of Mr Rugifer. However, Professor Dulcifer had been asked to make a reply, and his speech, too, was broadcast on all wavelengths.

BUT IT SEEMS TO ME THAT NOTHING COULD BE MORE UNHEALTHY....

'I have no hatred for the Fattypuffs,' he said. ('It isn't true,' said Edmund to Terry.) 'But it seems to me that nothing could be more unhealthy than to mix populations of different weight. We Thinifers owe our strength to our thinness. If we give it up we cannot tell what the future will bring.'

'There is something in that,' said Terry to his brother, and they began arguing just as they had done on the Surface.

The next day they learnt that the Fattypuff party had won. A lot of people in the country had voted for Dulcifer, but Rugifer was well ahead in Thiniville.

Edmund and Terry enjoyed themselves enormously during the weeks which followed. Passports had been done away with and nobody was weighed. The Fattypuffs could now travel freely across the Yellow Sea. They came by hundreds to Thiniville, bringing with them an atmosphere of gaiety and good-humour. Since they were allowed to preserve their ancient customs, special restaurants and cake-shops were opened to serve their hourly repasts. At first the older Thinifers viewed these innovations with such horror that a special Fattypuff quarter was instituted in the capital, where everybody weighing more than ten stone was obliged to live. But this part of the town became so popular that it only made things worse.

Edmund and Terry left Mr Dulcifer's house and rented a little flat together in the Fattypuff quarter. Lots of Thinifers invited their friends to spend the evening with them among the Fattypuffs. Special clinics for fattening sprang up, where the doctors guaranteed 'Two pounds gained every week. A Fattypuff in three months.' Fatness became popular among the Thinifer ladies, and those who couldn't manage to get fat wore enormous crinolines. Fattypuff plays were performed in all the theatres.

The craze was at its height when, three months after the plebiscite, ex-King Plumpapuff came to Thiniville.

He was travelling as a private citizen, but the Thinifers were so delighted to see a King, and especially such a fat one, that they treated him like a reigning monarch. When he went to the Opera the public demanded the 'Hymn to Plumpness' by Tumski-Korsapuff. Mr Rugifer and the King appeared together in a box, and were overwhelmed with applause.

The older Thinifers were increasingly worried. They had every reason to be, because, when in the following month a General Election was held in the two countries, the majority went to the Fattypuffs. The new Prime Minister was a Fattypuff, and Fattypuffs began to get all the best jobs, both in the government and in private business. At first the Thinifers were inclined to laugh at their slowness, their indolence and their inaccuracy in matters of detail, but presently they came to be preferred to the Thinifers in a large number of cases, particularly where it was a matter of ordering people about, because of their good humour, their staying power and the steadiness of their nerves. Terry, who had got Edmund a job in the Ministry for Slimming, saw him become first secretary while he himself remained second secretary.

One morning Terry ventured once again to question President Rugifer.

'And what are you going to do now, Mr Rugifer?' he asked.

'What about?' asked Mr Rugifer.

'To govern the country, which is getting more Fattypuff than King Plumpapuff himself.'

Mr Rugifer gave Terry's ear a friendly tug.

'Well, well,' he said, laughing. 'You're a babe and an innocent.'

The next morning placards surmounted by the crossed flags of Fattypuff and Thinifer informed the country:

(1) That King Plumpapuff was to be restored as sovereign of the United Kingdoms of Fattypuff and Thinifer.

(2) That the Ministry for Slimming was abolished, and that President Rugifer would become Chancellor of the United Kingdoms.

(3) That King Plumpapuff would have no power, and that the Thinifer constitution would continue in force.

The news was on the whole very well received, and in order to complete the general reconciliation it was decided that the Coronation ceremony should be held on the island which had been the cause of so much unhappiness. One problem still had to be solved, a problem so grave that people scarcely dared to mention it. What was to be the future name of the island? The conquering Thinifers could scarcely be expected to call it Fattyfer, nor could the King accept the name of

Thinipuff, so long rejected by his ancestors and detested by half his subjects. But to all questions Chancellor Rugifer replied:

'We may have confidence in the tact of His Majesty.'

The Royal Yacht set out for the Coronation with the question still unanswered. In official documents great care was taken to avoid naming the island.

When His Majesty landed it was covered by peach-trees in flower, their pink blossoms rippling like waves up the slopes of the hills. For some moments the King remained contemplating the scene with big, sleepy eyes. Standing beside him the Chancellor and the Ministers waited for him to speak.

'If we were to call it "Peachblossom Island"?' he said gently.

'Sire,' said Chancellor Rugifer, 'I never thought of that. I am a nincompoop and an idiot.'

12

The Return

SHORTLY after the Coronation festivities Chancellor Rugifer's two secretaries asked his permission to return to the Surface. They were far from being ill-treated, but they badly wanted to see their father and mother, who they feared would think them dead or lost in the forest. Perhaps the police had been sent all over the country in search of them. It was time to go home.

They had put off going for a long time because they felt they could be useful in helping to unite the Fattypuffs and the Thinifers, and certainly it had been a very good thing that the two brothers, one on each side, had been there to lend a hand. But now every thing was going well. King Plumpapuff and his Chancellor got along splendidly. Edmund and Terry could leave without

regrets. Chancellor Rugifer himself understood this. He pinched their ears and said:

'Gentlemen, you are ingrates and deserters!'

But all the same he ordered their passports to be got ready. He was even kind enough to allow them to make a last voyage to Fattyborough and to embark at Fattyport. Thus before leaving the Subterranean Kingdoms they had a last glimpse of the countries they had discovered.

The voyage to Fattyborough was most interesting. King Plumpapuff had kept his palace there, and he now passed six months of the year in each of his two capitals. The Fatty families had never forgiven him for what they described as his treachery. Professor Ramfatty was now at the head of a pure Fatty party which wished to re-establish absolute monarchy, and was trying to win over the King's son. The Professor dreamed of crowning the young man by the name of 'Superplump II'.

Edmund and Terry soon perceived, however, that the great majority of the Fattypuffs were satisfied with the new order of things. They still had their hourly meals and siestas. Their balloons floated happily in the air. They were content. Edmund, who went to visit his old friend ex-Chancellor Vorapuff, found him living serenely in a beautiful country retreat.

Prince Vorapuff took the two young Surface-dwellers to Fattyport in his private balloon car. The ruins caused by the War had been everywhere repaired. The light of the balloons was reflected in the gilt cupolas of the harbour. The crossing was delightful. When they reached Surface-by-the-Sea, Terry said to the Customs official:

'The Staircase to the Surface, please.'

'Have you passports?'

'Here they are.'

The official examined them carefully and said:

'All in order. I'll show you the way.'

He led them through the station by which they had arrived. They came to an opening like the mouth of a tunnel which was closed by an iron curtain. The official pressed a button, and the curtain rose.

There was the sound of machines, and the two brothers saw before them a staircase like the one which had brought them down. The official approached a grille and cried:

'Two Surface-dwellers. Two!' He did not add as formerly: 'One Fatty. One Thinny.' Distinctions by weight had been abolished for ever in the countries of the Underground.

The way up seemed endless. The boys' hearts were beating heavily. How would they find their parents? How would they get back from the forest to their home? On the Surface you needed money to travel. At length they saw above them, very far off, a speck of white light which slowly grew until it lit all the tunnel. It was the Surface.

They rushed wildly across the vast cavern lit by electric bulbs and found themselves at the foot of the Twin Rocks. And suddenly to their amazement they heard a voice calling:

'Hoi! hoi! HOI!'

It was their father.

They answered together at the tops of their voices:

'Hoi! hoi! HOI!'

They never knew how they managed to climb the chimney formed by the two pillars of the Twin Rocks. They scrambled up, using their backs and hands and feet, each pushing or pulling the other, breathless and exhausted, but joyful. Ten seconds later their two heads

appeared above the rock, and they saw their father standing below them. He was a little impatient, but not really angry.

'So there you are at last!' he said. 'I was getting quite worried.'

'But, Father!' said Terry. 'Do you mean to say you've been waiting for us all this time—ten months?'

'What!' cried Mr Double, laughing. 'Well, hardly ten months, but at least an hour.'

The fact is that in the kingdoms of the Underground, where there is neither sun nor moon, time goes exactly seven thousand times faster than it does on the Surface.

FATTYPUFFS

&

THINIFERS

The Backstory

Take the quiz to find out if you're a Fattypuff
or a Thinifer!

Who's Who in *Fattypuffs and Thinifers*

The Fattypuffs

Edmund Double: a Surface-dweller but without question a Fattypuff, Edmund adores food, just like his mother.

Mrs Double: Terry and Edmund's rather round mother.

Prince Vorapuff: the Chancellor of Fattypuff who Edmund meets on the boat. Edmund works for him as his secretary.

James Vorapuff: the Fattypuff chancellor's son.

King Plumpapuff XXXII: the King of the Fattypuffs, a most enormous man and very good-natured.

Marshal Puff: the greatest and most decorated soldier in the Fattypuff army.

Professor Ramfatty: President of the Academy of History, he is chosen to be one of the three delegates sent to the conference. For a Fattypuff he is considered quite bad tempered.

The Thinifers

Terry Double: a Surface-dweller but undoubtedly a Thinifer, Terry is not very interested in food and is as slender as his skinny father.

Mr Double: Terry and Edmund's rake-thin father.

Mr Dulcifer: Professor of History at the Thinifer National Academy who Terry meets on the boat to Thinifer and who he then goes to stay with.

President Rugifer: President of the National Council of Thinifer and the Minister of Slimming. Terry gets a job as his secretary. The President is very fiery and shouts insults at everyone but deep down he is good man.

Mrs Rugifer: President Rugifer's kind (and possibly slightly chubby) wife.

General Tactifer: the general in the Thinifer army, renowned for his strategic thinking.

Who was André Maurois?

André Maurois, whose real name was Emile Herzog, was
born in 1885 in France. His family owned a textile mill in
Elbeuf and André went to school in nearby Rouen. André's
childhood was not perfect – his parents were very formal
and restrained, and André sometimes found his hometown
too small and provincial. But he always felt at home there
and enjoyed seeing the river run different colours with the
millers' dyes and hearing the constant clatter of the mills.
And he had a good education which gave him a life-long
love of books and reading.

After school, André worked in the family mill for eight years
but he never stopped reading and practising his writing. He
also learnt to speak English very well. When the First World
War broke out André joined the French Army, and as he
could speak English he worked as an interpreter, serving
alongside the British Army. His first novel, published in
1918, was all about this experience and was very successful.

After the war André wrote more and more, alongside his
job running the mill, and eventually he was able to give up
his job to write full time. During the course of his career
he wrote many books including novels for both adults and

children, biographies and short stories. He also became a highly respected lecturer and speaker.

During the Second World War André worked as a captain in the French Army but after France was captured by Germany he moved to America and worked on anti-Nazi propaganda. After the war, he moved back to France and continued his very successful career as a writer. André died in 1967.

A message fom Fritz Wegner, the illustrator

I still remember the thrill and excitement when in 1968
Judy Taylor, who was then publisher of children's books at
The Bodley Head, commissioned me to illustrate André
Maurois' ingenious story 'Fattypuffs and Thinifers'. It gave
me the opportunity to test my invention and humour, the
two ingredients I most wanted to bring to my drawings.
Looking at those illustrations of twenty-five years ago I still
sense the pleasure of interpreting the underground world
of the plump, amiable and lazy Fattypuffs (my favourites)
being drawn into conflict with the lean, fussy and energetic
Thinifers. Although the Fattypuffs lost the war to the more
organized, precision-minded Thinifers, the subsequent
reconciliation served to give them a much better mutual
understanding. It is a tale of the two nations whose hostility
for each other is due to conflicting lifestyles resulting in a
bitter struggle for supremacy.

André Maurois tells the story with irony and good humour,
but I suspect we 'surface-dwellers' are meant to draw some
revealing moral conclusions.

Fattypuffs v. Thinifers: the war

As well as being a hilarious tale about a crazy, made-up world, this book is also a story about war. What do you think is the message about war in *Fattypuffs and Thinifers*? The consequences of the battles in this story are terrible – people are hurt and killed, and beautiful, unique cities are bombed and destroyed. In the end though, the two sides are united, so perhaps the war was worth it. What do you think? Ponder these questions, if you will . . .

- Do you think it was right for the Fattypuffs and the Thinifers to remain firm over the ownership and name of Peachblossom Island?

- How do you think the two sides could have avoided the war?

- Do you side with the Fattypuffs or the Thinifers? Why?

- If you had been leading one of the armies, do you think you would have declared all-out war?

- What do you think André Maurois's message was when he wrote this book?

Have you thought about it yet? Well, here's some more food for thought – some people think that Fattypuff and Thinifer represent real countries: France and Germany. The Fattypuffs are the French, with their love of good food, and the Thinifers are the efficient Germans.

France and Germany certainly have had a rocky history and have fought many wars against each other. A few years before André's birth his family had to flee their home during the Franco-Prussian War (1870–71), where France and Germany were pitted against one another. When the First World War occurred, once again the two countries were on opposing sides – a brutal conflict that André witnessed firsthand. Later on, nine years after the publication of *Fattypuffs and Thinifers*, the Second World War brought the two countries into conflict once again. Was André using this crazy story to make a very important point? And what do you think his hopes were for the future of Europe?

'You are a half-wit and a nincompoop!' Or are you? Test your knowledge of *Fattypuffs and Thinifers*

(Turn to the back for answers. No cheating!)

1) There is no sunshine under the earth so how is the world of the Fattypuffs and Thinifers lit?

2) What is the capital of Thinifer?

3) What is the capital of Fattypuff?

4) What is the name of the desert in the countries under the earth?

5) What is the favourite breed of dog in Thinifer?

6) What tax did King Plumpapuff abolish when he became king?

7) What does Edmund accidentally call King Plumpapuff when he first meets him?

8) Which character loves trains and railways?

9) How often do the Fattypuffs eat?

10) What new name is given in the end to the Island of Fattyfer or Thinipuff?

The Fattypuff all-time favourite snack! The classic French delicacy! Indulge your inner Fattypuff and learn to make . . . CREAM BUNS

First make the 'choux' (pronounced shoe) pastry buns

What you'll need:

120ml water
20g caster sugar
100g butter
1 teaspoon salt
120g plain flour
4 eggs, beaten
A helpful adult on hand

1)   Gently heat the water, sugar, butter and salt in a large pan. Bring to the boil and then quickly add the flour, all at once. Turn the heat to low and beat the mixture vigorously for about a minute. Then turn it out on to a plate greased with a bit of butter and leave to cool.

2)   Meanwhile pre-heat your oven to 220°C/425°F/Gas Mark 7.

3) When the dough is at room temperature, put it back in the pan and gradually beat in the eggs (not on the hob or you'll make doughy scrambled eggs). The dough should become smooth and glossy.

4) Butter a baking tray and spoon large blobs of dough on to it (about 10 of them). Make sure they're spaced well apart.

5) Turn the oven down to 200°C/400°F/Gas Mark 6 and bake for 20 minutes. The buns should come out big, airy and golden.

Next, make the filling . . . crème pâtissière (a kind of creamy custard)

What you'll need:

½ vanilla pod
500ml milk
50g plain flour
75g caster sugar
I egg
3 egg yolks

1) Run the point of a knife along the vanilla pod to split it open and scrape out the seeds inside, into a large saucepan. Chuck the pod into the pan too.

2)   Add the milk and slowly bring to the boil.

3)   Mix the flour, sugar, egg and egg yolks in a bowl.

4)   When the vanilla milk has boiled, pour it onto the mixture in the bowl a little at a time, stirring constantly.

5)   When it's all mixed in, put the whole mixture back into the saucepan and cook over a gentle heat, stirring all the time. Don't stop stirring even for a second!

6)   The moment the mixture comes to the boil and starts to thicken, take it off the heat. Take out the vanilla pod and leave to cool. Then put it in the fridge to chill.

To make your cream buns:

1)   Make a horizontal slit in each pastry bun, as if you're cutting off a lid.

2)   Gently lever the bun open and spoon in a big, generous blob of crème pâtissière.

3)   And they're done. Ta-daaa!

Who are you?
Are you a chilled-out fatty or an efficient thinny? Take the quiz to find out . . .

1) **Which shape do you prefer?**

    a)   Circle

    b)   Triangle

    c)   Heart

    d)   Square

2) **Do you love to sleep?**

    a)   Yes

    b)   No

3) **Which activity do you like the most?**

    a)   Running

    b)   Reading

    c)   Playing war games

4) **Are you more likely to be found . . .**

    a)   Snuggled under the duvet

    b)   Jumping on the bed

5) **What would you prefer to eat?**

   a) Spaghetti
   b) Éclair
   c) Spaghetti followed by éclair

6) **How do you solve an argument with another person?**

   a) Talk gently to calm them down
   b) Talk firmly to make them see reason

7) **Are you a bit bossy?**

   a) No
   b) Yes

8) **Which word sounds better to you?**

   a) Balloon
   b) Twig
   c) Chomp
   d) Whip

Scores:

1)a)3, b)1, c)4, d)2. **2)**a)3, b)2. **3)**a)1, b)3, c)2. **4)**a)4, b)1.
5)a)2, b)3, c)4. **6)**a)4, b)1. **7)**a)4, b)1. **8)**a)3, b)2, c)4, d)1.

The Results . . .

10–20 points: You are a speedy, sharp thinifer! Whether you're a skinny mini or a chubby cherub you intend to pack as much action into your life as possible. Smart, organised and active, you know how to get things done – wasting time is for absolute nincompoops!

20–30 points: You are a great enormous Fattypuff! Whether you're fat or thin, one thing's for certain: the laid-back life is for you. Jolly, friendly and fun – your belief is that life is to be enjoyed.

What does that word mean?

Adding-machine – a type of old-fashioned, mechanical calculator

Annex – to take over neighbouring land by force and add it to your own land

Armistice – when two warring parties agree to stop fighting

Coronation – the ceremony to crown a new king or queen

Crinoline – a big skirt with a hoop underneath to hold out the fabric

Cupola – a small dome on the roof of a building

Debouch – to march from a narrow place into a wide, open area

Delegates – people chosen to represent others in a meeting or at a conference

Dignitary – a high-ranking, important person

Frontier – an international border

Indolent – always lazy and unwilling to do much

Ingrate – an ungrateful person

Oriflamme – a bright red banner, given to French Kings in the old days when they set off to war

Paul Pry – a nosy person (from a character in an 1826 play called *Paul Pry*)

Pennant – a flag

Plebiscite – like a referendum, where the people are asked to vote about a particular issue

Sortie – an armed attack

Answers to the *Fattypuffs and Thinifers* quiz – how did you do?

1) It is lit by huge luminous balloons floating in the sky

2) Thiniville

3) Fattyborough

4) The Desert of Sandypuff

5) The greyhound

6) The tax on Turkish delight

7) Humpty-Dumpty

8) Edmund

9) Every hour

10) Peachblossom Island

Visit **www.worldofstories.co.uk**